D1435886

BLUE RIDGE LIBRARY
28 AVERY ROW
ROANOKE, VIRGINIA 24012-8500

There are lots of fun things to do at the Manor. You can stroll through the cemetery, watch the swamp glow under the moonlight or make a few new friends!

The FEMUR Family

EYE-GORE & STEVE

This sweet little family may look scary, but the truth is that they have no guts at all.

They want to be skate punks, but they're really just zombies with bad attitudes.

BEATRICE Mon Staire

...e's haunted by a horrible ...cret...and a hairdo ...at's even worse.

Wolf Man STU

When the moon is full, he becomes human. Well, *somewhat* human...

COUNT SNOBULA

He isn't rich, but he *is* totally stuck up. Thank goodness he sleeps all day.

Step through the gate—
let's see who's home!

The SWAMP HORROR

SALLY the Specter

Professor VON SKALPEL

It ain't easy being a big green ball of toxic slime!

Beatrice's mother is smart, sassy—and a ghost!

The most brilliant m scientist in town. He's a real cutup.

FRANKIE

Created by Von Skalpel,
Frankie is one of a kind.
Thank goodness.

Take a look inside the Manor.
It might be old, but the monsters
think of it as "home, sweet home."

Von Skalp
Room

Th
Se

V

The
Femur Crypt

Eye-Gore
and
Steve's Pit

The Radioactive Swamp

Watch out, or Horror might want to show you his home!

CHAPTER ONE
Hip, Hip, Horror!

"Hurry up," one of the workmen whispered as he looked over at the house that sat on the hill nearby. "I don't want to be here after dark."

"Monster Manor gives me the creeps," the other workman agreed, using the nickname the villagers of Transylvaniaville had made up for the house. Its real name was Mon Staire Manor, but everyone called it Monster Manor, because horrible creatures lived there. "I'm leaving the minute the sun goes down."

"You'll be here as long as it takes to lay the pipes," boomed a voice behind them.

The workmen turned and saw a scary figure in dark glasses and an overcoat. He was frowning sternly at them.

"Sorry, Mr. Pitt!" one of the men said. "We didn't hear you drive up."

"You'll lay the pipes tonight," Pitt went on. "Or all of you will find yourselves new jobs. Understood?"

"Yes, Mr. Pitt," the workmen chorused.

"Besides," Pitt added as the men hurried about their work. "I understand those monsters are pretty harmless. Which is why I have such high hopes for them. . . ."

It's No-More-Slime-Time.

Shrieks and shouts poured out from the Manor. There were loud thumpings and the sound of jaws tearing into food and lips smacking. What was going on? Had the monsters found some new victim?

Actually, no. They were having a party.

"Hand me another one of those bugs-on-a-stick," Wolf Man Stu said to Steve, one of the two zombies who lived in the cemetery behind the Manor.

Count Snobula, the snooty old vampire, smacked his lips as he poured himself another glass of punch. (*Vampire* punch, if you know what I mean.) "Delicious!" he said. He chugged the whole glass and let out a delicate belch. The count was a very classy guy.

Tibia Femur, one of the skeletons, handed her daughter, Kneecap, a barbecued rib.

"Mom, I want one, too!" cried Bonehead, Kneecap's brother. "They're delithiouth!" Bonehead had a horrible lisp.

"Settle down, there's plenty for everyone," Fibula Femur, the little skeletons' father, insisted.

Steve's brother, Eye-Gore, passed around a plate of mini–grasshopper tarts. One of Eye-Gore's eyeballs had just fallen into the tart. "Sorry," he said, as Professor Von Skalpel, the mad scientist, took one. The professor picked the eye out and bit into the tart as Eye-Gore popped his eye back into place.

"Scrumptious!" the professor said. He was not easily grossed out. After all, he put monsters together for fun!

Frankie, a monster that the professor had sewn together out of body parts dug up from the local cemetery, turned the music up, and Wolf Man Stu dragged Beatrice Mon Staire— the owner of the Manor—onto the dance floor. She frowned at him, but ended up dancing, anyway. For a witch, Beatrice could be a decent person. . . . when she felt like it.

Suddenly, Von Skalpel turned the music down. "I vould like to propose a toast!" the professor said in his strange accent, which he claimed was from southern New Jersey. "To zee birzday boy!" Professor Von Skalpel gestured to an enormous ball of oozing green slime.

The green slime smiled shyly. "Thank you all," said the Swamp Horror. "This means so much to me."

"Speech! Speech!" called Count Snobula.

Horror cleared his throat. "Ten years ago, I was a timid little thing who couldn't tie its own shoelace without falling into a radioactive swamp. Who would have thought that one minute of sheer klutziness would bring me here—to my best friends? Every birthday since then has been a happy one." With that, he wrapped them all in a monster-sized hug.

"Er—you're squishing me," Wolf Man Stu griped.

"And you're getting slime on my silk cape," Count Snobula said.

"I just love you guys!" Horror sang.

"Seriously," Beatrice added. "You can put us down now."

Horror set his friends down gently and grinned. "Thanks for the party," he said. "You're the best friends ever."

"Hear, hear," the professor cried, and all of the monsters burst into applause. Steve clapped so hard that his hand fell off and flew

right into Count Snobula's drink with a loud *plop*!

Beatrice dimmed the lights, and a moment later her mother, Sally—the only ghost in the Manor—floated into the room carrying a large platter heaped with greenish sludge. "It's my specialty," Sally said. "Toxic Waste Delight."

The monsters oohed and aahed over the delicious-looking dish.

Sally put the plate in front of Horror and handed him a cake knife. "In your horror—I mean, honor," Sally said.

Just then, the Toxic Waste Delight began to jiggle. Then it let out a croak!

Horror frowned. "What's this?" he asked.

Sally beamed. "The surprise!"

Horror poked at the dessert with his knife, and suddenly, a disgusting, six-eyed toad flopped out.

"That's revolting!" Horror cried, staring at the hideous creature. "I can't believe you put Willy in a dessert!"

Quickly, Willy leaped from the table onto Bonehead's skull, which made all of the monsters crack up. All of them except Horror, that is. Willy was his favorite pet, and he didn't want him to get away.

Willy let out a loud *ribbit*, then jumped onto Count Snobula's plate. Horror caught the mutant frog and picked him up.

"Would everyone please stop putting their hands all over my meal?"

Ribbit.

the count complained out loud.

"Don't worry, Willy," Horror whispered to the deformed toad. "I'll take care of you."

"Oh, rats," Sally said as she watched the swamp thing hurry from the Manor, leaving his party behind. "I thought it would be so cute to have a froggie jump out of the cake."

CHAPTER TWO
Free Willy

The swamp glowed green under the moon-light. Actually, it glowed green pretty much all of the time, whether the moon was out or not, thanks to the chemicals that were pumped into it by GPC, a nearby company.

"It's okay, don't worry," Horror whispered to Willy as he dipped him into the slimy, radioactive swamp water. "Everything's going to be okay. Take a little sip."

Willy slurped up some sludgy water, then

heaved a huge sigh. Horror smiled. He could tell that his little friend was feeling better already. "Now we need to get you some dinner," Horror said. He splashed around the swamp, looking for bugs and worms.

"Can we help?"

Horror looked up and saw Bonehead and Kneecap standing nearby. Bonehead reached out to pet Willy, and the mutant frog licked the skeleton's hand with a big, slurping, blue tongue.

"Mom didn't want us to follow you," Kneecap told Horror. "She said that the swamp was full of gross, scary beasts. But we were worried about Willy."

Horror climbed out of the mud. He put a pile of worms on an old Frisbee that had been left in the swamp back before it had become polluted, and handed the platter to Bonehead.

"You can feed him if you want," Horror said.

Bonehead and Kneecap took turns handing Willy the worms, one by one.

"Thith ith totally dithguthting!" Bonehead said as he fed another slimy worm to the frog. "Awethome!"

"See?" Horror said as he gave Willy a pat. "The swamp creatures aren't scary at all. Gross, maybe, but not scary. Let me show you something." Horror picked up an old bottle that was lying at the edge of the swamp.

"Aieee!" Kneecap cried as a giant tentacle came out of the bottle and grabbed her. It lifted her off the ground and gave her a shake, rattling her bones, and then it disappeared back into the bottle as quickly as it had sprung out.

"Sorry!" Horror cried as he and Bonehead hurried to try to put Kneecap together again. "Coco isn't usually so grumpy!"

"Did you break anything?" Bonehead asked his sister.

"No, I don't think so," Kneecap said. Bonehead had attached her arm bone to her elbow bone, and she reached up to rub her skull. "But I lost my pink ribbon. I think it fell into

Sorry, kids!

I guess I'm all bottled up!

the swamp when that creature shook me."

"That's strange," Horror said, rubbing his chin. "Coco usually only sticks out her tentacle when she's afraid of something."

"Did I scare her?" Kneecap asked.

"I don't think so," Horror said. "You're too small to give Coco a scare. It must have been something else. . . ."

"Ribbit," Willy said. All six of his bulging, froggy eyes were staring at the end of the swamp. Horror followed his gaze, and let out a gasp.

"What'th wrong?" Bonehead said, staring at the swamp. "The thwamp lookths perfectly fine to me."

"That's right!" Horror cried. "The swamp is . . . *fine!*"

It was true. Half of the swamp wasn't glowing at all. In fact, it was burbling with pure, clear water. There was no doubt about it—the radioactive swamp was disappearing before their very eyes, leaving nothing behind but a beautiful, crystal-clear lake. A trickle of water flowed over the bank and lapped at Horror's big toe.

"Yikes!" Horror shouted, leaping away from the swamp's edge. "Get it away from me!"

The toad was looking even worse than usual. He was sprawled in the middle of the clean water, shivering and coughing.

"That pure water will kill him!" Horror shouted. "We have to get him into some pollution before it's too late! We have to get all of the swamp creatures back into the sludge! Help me collect it before it all disappears!"

"I'll go get some buckets!" Kneecap said.

"I'll come, too!" Bonehead shouted, running after his sister.

"Hurry, kids!" Horror shouted as he stared at his froggy friend, who was trapped in the beautiful lake. "We have to free Willy!"

CHAPTER THREE
Things Get Gooey

"Give me thirty cc's of slime, STAT!" Horror shouted as he hurried toward the Manor with Willy.

"I never should have served that frog for dessert," Sally wailed, as she passed a pot full of slime to Frankie.

The monsters had formed a bucket brigade to pass polluted water up to the Manor. Kneecap and Bonehead filled a pot at the edge of the marsh, then handed the pot off to Steve, who gave the pot to Beatrice, who gave the pot to Sally, who gave the pot to Frankie, who gave the pot to Eye-Gore, who gave the pot to Count Snobula, who put the pot down so that Horror could come and collect it once he had finished helping Willy. The monsters gathered the sludge in everything they could think of— the professor's organ jars, trash cans, buckets, and pasta pots.

"I guess I won't be cooking pasta for a while," Beatrice said, as one of her best pots, now covered in glowing, green slime, passed under her nose.

"Schtop schpilling!" Professor Von Skalpel commanded, inspecting the bucket brigade. "Don't you know how to handle a zoup tureen?" he asked Count Snobula.

"I always had servants to do that," the count replied, with his nose in the air.

The professor turned to Wolf Man Stu. "Zat trash can isn't full," he barked.

Stu dumped the contents of the can onto the professor's head.

"Hmmm," the professor said, as slime dripped all over his clothes. "Actually, I guess it vas pretty full, after all."

By the time Horror reported that Willy was feeling much better, the monsters had collected as much radioactive waste as they could.

"Thank you, my friends!" Horror shouted.

"I think Willy will be all right. And now I'm going to try to rescue some of the other swamp creatures before it's too late."

"Great," growled Wolf Man Stu. "I'm going upstairs to take a shower." His fur was completely matted with green slime.

"No way, dog chow!" squealed Steve. "Me first!"

"Since I am the senior member of this group," Count Snobula declared, "and have an extremely large amount of slime on my cape, I think that I should—"

All of the other monsters darted past him, racing for the bathroom.

"—Go first," Count Snobula finished. "Hey—wait up!" he called as he followed them up the stairs.

Eye-Gore, who was in the lead, had almost reached the top when his leg fell off. Wolf Man

Stu leaped over him and yanked open the bathroom door with a triumphant cry.

"Ha-ha!" Wolf Man Stu said. "See you, suckers!" But when he turned to go into the bathroom, he let out a howl.

The bathroom was covered in sludge. It looked as though there were more green slime in there than there had been in all of the radioactive swamp.

"*Ribbit,*" said Willy, from his place in the sink. The bathtub was full of slime, clearly waiting to become a home for more swamp creatures.

Just then, Horror walked in with a two-headed fish, which he plopped into the tub. "There you go!" Horror chirped to the fish, which quickly disappeared beneath the green murk.

"And just how am I going to get the sludge

BLUE RIDGE LIBRARY
28 AVERY ROW
ROANOKE, VIRGINIA 24012-8500

out of my fur?" Wolf Man Stu grumbled.

Horror shrugged. "Garden hose?" he suggested. "If that doesn't work, try the sprinkler. I'll see you later. I have to go save Coco before she gets clean."

With a look of determination, Horror set off to find Coco, slamming the door shut behind him.

CHAPTER FOUR
Whirl World

The monsters were extremely cranky the next morning.

"You smell like slime," Wolf Man Stu said to Count Snobula.

"Well, I'm too polite to tell you what you smell like," the count shot back.

"Enough!" Beatrice shouted. "We all smell horrible, but there's nothing we can do about it until the swamp creatures move out of the bathroom." With that, she snapped on the TV.

The chirpy music of *The Chit-Chat Show* floated into the room. All of the monsters gathered around the television set.

"I hate this show," Wolf Man Stu griped as he pulled his chair closer to the TV. Everyone ignored him.

"Good morning!" The show's hostess, Patty Cake, beamed into the camera. "Today we are going live on location to interview Mr. D. K. Pitt, owner of GPC. Terry? What have you got to tell us?"

The audience clapped as the camera cut to a remote location, where the interviewer—Terry Gator—held a microphone up to a scowling man in dark glasses.

"Good morning," Pitt said in a sour voice. He didn't look as if he were having a very good morning.

"Now, Mr. Pitt," Terry said. "Tell us about your new project."

"I've decided to build a brand-new water park," Pitt said. "It's going to be the ultimate in family fun."

"What does *that* guy know about fun?" Steve asked. "He doesn't even smile." The others shushed him.

"It's going to be on the long-abandoned Mon Staire site," Pitt went on.

"What?" everyone cried. Everyone, that is, except the professor, who cried, "Vhat?"

"That's right, I'm going to clean up the Mon Staire site and build the most amazing water park," Pitt repeated.

"But isn't GPC responsible for polluting that particular area?" Terry Gator asked.

"GPC is also responsible for creating a super-high-tech pollution *cleaner*," Pitt said. "Now, we can take swamp water and make it clean enough to drink."

"But too clean for a poor six-eyed toad!" Horror cried. "So that's what's happening to the swamp—Mr. Pitt is ruining it!"

"Not only that," Pitt went on, "but we have created an amazing new building tool—the Bulldosaur. This machine will make the Radioactive Swamp into a paradise on earth!"

"I can't believe this," Fibula Femur said as the interview ended and Patty Cake moved on to talking about salad. "We're going to be stuck right in the middle of paradise!"

"This is awful," Frankie moaned.

"How dare he!" Beatrice shouted. "That man can't just move onto my property! I'm calling my lawyer!"

Horror sighed and walked outside to inspect the swamp. Outside the Manor, workmen were already putting up a huge sign that said, "Whirl World Water

Park." But the worst part was the swamp itself. The last of Horror's poor little swampy friends had been driven out by a pair of nasty white swans, which swam across the now-blue lake as though they owned the place. There were trees, pink gravel, and tufts of green grass—and even two dolphins jumping around in the lake! Only a small section of swamp—near the island in the center of the water—was left.

Horror shook his head. "There goes the neighborhood," he said.

CHAPTER FIVE
Bulldosaur

Suddenly, a loud roar sounded from across the lake. Horror looked in the direction of the noise and saw a giant machine with sharp, snapping jaws headed for the edge of the swamp. It rolled forward, scooped up a mouthful of chemical dirt in its mouth, and then dumped it into a tank in the rear. The tank sorted out the polluted swamp earth and shook the dirt around until it came out of the machine as sparkly, pink gravel.

"Oh, no! The Bulldosaur!" Horror cried. "I have to get my treasures right away!"

Horror's "treasures" were really just a few things that any other person would have called junk and thrown away years before. But those things were special to Horror, and he had sealed them in a small box and buried them in a puddle of quicksand on the island at the center of the swamp.

Horror dived into the lake and swam to his island. *"Bleugh!"* he shouted, as he ran out, shaking off the clean water. *"Puh! Puh! Puh!"* Some of the water had seeped into his mouth, and he was trying to spit it out. *Dis*-gusting.

Reaching into the puddle of quicksand, Horror pulled out his tin box. Everything was just as he had left it—his battered old trumpet, on which he liked to play the big hits of the 1980s, a lottery ticket that had two of the seven winning numbers, a toy pistol that played a funny song when you pulled the trigger, and an old photograph. Horror took the photo out of the plastic bag and smiled at it sadly. It was of a man with a lopsided grin and a mop of dark, curly hair. In the picture, his shoelaces were untied, and it was clear that he was about to trip over them. It was a picture of Horror, the way he used to be—before he had fallen into the swamp.

A loud chirping erupted from the other side

of the swamp, and Horror looked up to see that the Bulldosaur was headed toward a pair of swamp birds. Well, they seemed to be birds, even though they had three eyes each, and didn't have any feathers, just wrinkly skin, like that of plucked chickens. They did, however, have beaks. And one of the birds was sitting on a nest, which Horror saw was full of eggs.

"Ha-ha-ha!" The man behind the machine laughed evilly. Horror realized that it was D. K. Pitt himself—and that he was aiming for the birds and the nest!

"Don't worry, birdies, I'm coming!" Horror shouted as he jumped into the lake with a giant splash. He crawled out of the water and leaped in front of the birds. "Stop!" he hollered. "You'll squish those birds over my dead body!"

"Sounds good to me," Pitt said. He revved up the machine and moved it with surprising speed straight toward Horror.

Pitt was unaware that the swamp had changed Horror in many ways. The best, by far, of those changes was the fact that, ever since he had fallen into the radioactive water, he had become incredibly graceful. Horror

grabbed the birds and the eggs, and rolled onto the ground like a blob of jelly. He put the birds and their eggs onto a low branch of a nearby tree, and then bounced against the side of the Bulldosaur and stuck there, with a heavy, wet *splat*!

"Tweet! Tweet!" said the swamp birds, which translated into, "Get him, Blobby!"

Horror clung to the door with his right hand and held on to his box of treasures with his left. Pitt growled and flicked a few levers. Suddenly, the jaws of the Bulldosaur moved and headed straight for Horror!

"I'm going to recycle you into some sparkly, pink gravel!" Pitt shouted.

But the Bulldosaur couldn't hold on to Horror's slimy skin. Pitt snarled and pushed all of the levers and buttons on the panel in front of him.

"You'll never catch me!" Horror shouted. "I'm too smooth!"

Just then, there was a clanking sound, and Horror felt himself lifted into the air. The Bulldosaur had attached itself to the tin box, and was now dangling Horror over the recycling tank. Horror had no choice. He swung away and dived into the lake, leaving his treasures behind.

He heard a metallic thunk as the box fell into the tank.

I'm about to become a smoothie!

CHAPTER SIX
Endangered Manor

"*T*hief!" Beatrice cried. "It's impossible! Im! Poss! Ih! Bel!" She shouted each syllable distinctly. "I'll get whoever did this!"

Horror looked toward the Manor. Could it be that Beatrice knew what happened to him, and wanted to help? He hurried toward the Manor and ran up to Beatrice's room. She was standing with Professor Von Skalpel.

"Did you see?" Horror asked. "Are you going to make that meanie give me back all of my treasures?" Horror held his breath.

"What?" Beatrice cried. "What treasures?"

"Beatrice has just found zee deed to zee Manor," the professor explained. "It seems zat she owns zee house, but not zee land surrounding it."

"What does that mean?" Horror asked. Legal-speak didn't make much sense to the swamp creature. He was more of a history and literature buff.

"It means zat D. K. Pitt can build vhatever he vants on zee land outside the Manor," Professor Von Skalpel said. "As long as he has permission from zee people who own it."

Hearing this, Horror burst into great, big, slobbery, boo-hoo tears. Now he would never get his box back. And his swamp friends would have to live in the bathroom. And all of his monster friends would smell like slime for-

ever! He shook with the force of his sobs.

The professor and Beatrice took a few steps back. It wasn't smart to stand near Horror when he was crying. Green, slimy tears poured from his eyes and splattered all over the floor.

"Frankie!" Professor Von Skalpel shouted. "Please come here!" Frankie was his assistant, and the professor often made him take care of whatever messes needed cleaning up.

"And bring a mop!" Beatrice added.

As Horror boo-hooed his head off, Beatrice sighed. "Who would have been dumb enough to sell our land?" she muttered.

"Dumb?" shrieked a voice. Sally poked her head through the ceiling. She was a ghost—she could do stuff like that. She floated down and began shouting at her daughter. "Do you think your father's sorcerer's income was enough to live on? No way! I sold the land before I died—and I got a good price for it, too!"

"But the land has been in the family for centuries!" Beatrice shouted.

"So what?" Sally asked. "That just means it was old! If you want some land, go buy yourself some-thing new."

Christmas 1985—How do you think we were able to buy you the Barbie Dreamhouse?

"Well, do you at least remember who bought the land?" Beatrice asked.

"Yes," the professor went on. "Maybe ve can ask zis person to tell Mr. Pitt to stop his project. Maybe ve can raise zee money and buy zee land back!"

"I sold it to some guy in dark glasses," Sally said. "His name was Douglass Kimball Pitt."

The professor and Beatrice looked at each other as Horror burst into a new round of sobs. Sally rolled her eyes and then disappeared.

"Could you cast a spell on Mr. Pitt?" the professor asked Beatrice. "Maybe you could use magic to change his mind."

"Hmmm . . ." Beatrice said, pretending to think it over. The truth was, she was lousy at magic. She had flunked out of witchcraft school. But she didn't really want anyone else to know that. "The water park opens tomorrow," she said. "If I use magic on Mr. Pitt, everyone will realize I am a witch."

"Good point," the professor said. The villagers in Transylvaniaville weren't particularly fond of witches.

"Maybe we should go with the more . . . scientific approach," Beatrice suggested.

The professor lifted his eyebrows. "I'm listening."

"You have so many inventions," Beatrice said. "Can't you use one of them to—uh—get rid of Mr. Pitt and his workmen?"

Perhaps . . .

Perhaps ve could feed him zis radioactive cheddar!

"Vhy, of course!" Professor Von Skalpel replied. "Frankie—finish up zat mopping, and come viz me!"

"What should I do with these?" Frankie asked, holding out the two featherless swamp birds, which had followed Horror into the room.

Horror, whose sobs had turned to sniffles, collected the birds and took them into the bathroom so they could be with the other swamp creatures.

The professor hurried down to his laboratory. There was no time to lose!

CHAPTER SEVEN
Land of Wonder

"**W**here are we going?" Frankie asked, as the professor led him through the Manor gate. Then he yawned. Frankie and the professor had been up all night, searching the laboratory for something that might stop D. K. Pitt. At one point, Beatrice had even come down to help, but even with her help, they hadn't found anything that worked.

"To zee vater park," the professor said.

"Oooh—can I go on the big slide?" Frankie

asked excitedly. He loved slides.

"No," the professor snapped. "You have to try to blend in viz zee crowd. Ve are going to schpy on Mr. Pitt, and zee how his vater park operates. Zen, maybe ve can find a vay to schtop him."

Professor Von Skalpel paid for the tickets to the park, and handed one to Frankie. "Just remember," the professor said, looking him up and down. "Try to blend in."

"No problem," Frankie said as he barreled through the gate, accidentally ripping it off its hinges. "Oops."

The professor rolled his eyes. Maybe this hadn't been such a good idea, after all. He bought Frankie some cotton candy, then suggested that they split up and search in different areas.

"You look around zee lake," the professor

said. "And I'll look in zee gift shop and at zee dolphin show." Actually, the professor was just really eager to see the dolphin show. Whirl, the dolphin, was the major attraction at the park.

In fact, the professor noticed, as he began to walk around the park, Whirl was everywhere. People were wearing Whirl sunglasses, and carrying stuffed Whirl dolls, licking Whirl lollipops, and wearing Whirl T-shirts. The gift shop offered a huge array of Whirl merchandise: beach towels, cameras, suntan lotion, panty hose, and even toilet paper—everything bore a picture of the happy dolphin.

"I guess zere aren't any clues in here," the professor said as he headed outside. The dolphin show was about to start, anyway. And he wanted to get a good seat.

The sign outside said that Whirl would juggle balls, jump through hoops, and pull his trainer on water skis. After the intermission, he would waltz with a spectator, perform the famous "To Be or Not to Be" speech from *Hamlet*, and land a flaming helicopter.

"Sounds like a great show," the professor said, as he headed over to the water tank. But as he peered at the dolphin, the professor had to admit that Whirl didn't look so good. In fact,

WHIRL

TICKETS

Is zere a mad-scientist discount?

Whirl looked as if he might hurl. His dolphin tank was full of the Whirl toys that were sold in the gift shop. The professor pulled out a small, blue, plastic, toy dolphin and looked at it thoughtfully. Then he slipped it into his pocket and sat down to watch the show.

The professor had to admit that the show was pretty incredible, even though Whirl was clearly feeling ill. "I have seen better readings of *Hamlet*," the professor remarked, to no one in particular, as he left. Still, the dolphin had landed the helicopter with only one fin, which was pretty impressive.

The rest of the park was still under construction. So after the show, there wasn't much to do.

"I vonder vhat Frankie thinks of the water schlides," the professor grumbled as he walked away from the rides. None of them were finished yet, and they didn't look as though they would be very exciting when they were. There weren't any loop-de-loop roller coasters, or rides where one had to escape from a giant tidal wave, or scary tunnels full of love. There were just baby-sized, train-style rides.

Zis place needs a little jazzing up, the professor remarked to

WHIRL

That's Vhirl?

Yeah, he's not looking too lively.

Do not feed peanuts to Whirl!

Hey, you!

Hliiik

Maybe we should stop feeding him donuts.

himself. Except for the dolphin show, there really wasn't much to do.

The professor poked around, looking for Frankie. After a while, he figured that the creature must have headed home, and Professor Von Skalpel decided to do the same. He didn't think that he had found anything useful, but he wanted to tell Beatrice about what he had seen, anyway. He headed out the gate and started walking up toward the Manor.

Just then, a voice boomed over the loud-speaker. "Don't miss our brand-new, surprise attraction, 'House of Horror.' You'll scream in terror when you see the amazingly lifelike monsters!"

House of Horror? the professor repeated to himself. Vhat does a haunted house have to do 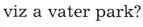 viz a vater park?

CHAPTER EIGHT
House of Horror!

"What's going on?" the professor asked as he walked up to Monster Manor. A crowd of people stood outside the gate. The professor had seen crowds of angry villagers outside the Manor before, but these people didn't look angry. In fact, they looked as though they were waiting for something. The professor elbowed his way to the front of the crowd.

"Excuse me," said a man wearing a Whirl shirt and a Whirl cap. He held up his hand to stop the professor. "I'm sorry, but the House of Horror will not be open for another five minutes."

"But zis isn't zee House of Horror," the professor said. "It's vhere I li—"

That's when it hit him. D. K. Pitt was trying to make Monster Manor into part of his theme park!

"You'll never get in!" Beatrice shouted as she shook her fist at the crowd that had gathered outside the Manor gate. "We are not freaks to be stared at!"

"Really, this is most embarrassing," Count Snobula griped.

"Look, Bonehead," Kneecap said as she peered out the window. "We're famous!"

"Leth go meet our public," Bonehead said, and the two little skeletons headed outside. They were both very excited. It wasn't every day that they got to see real, live human beings.

"Maybe we can even scare a few of them," Kneecap suggested.

"I'm way ahead of you," Bonehead agreed, giving the crowd a ghoulish grin. He moaned loudly, and waved his hands threateningly toward the crowd.

The crowd let out a loud "Oooh!" and a few flashbulbs popped.

"Very realistic," one woman said.

"Oh, puh-leeze." Her teenage daughter rolled her eyes. "That thing is so fake. I could make a better skeleton out of chicken wire and paper-towel tubes."

Kneecap was a little disappointed, but Bonehead kept on with his scary skeleton routine. After a while, Kneecap got a little bored, and looked over toward the lake. She just

wished that she could find her pink ribbon. She felt naked without it.

"Booga-booga-booga!" Bonehead shouted at the crowd.

"Ahhh," they said. And then they snapped more photos.

"You call that scary?" said a voice behind them.

Bonehead and Kneecap turned to see Eye-Gore standing behind them. "Stand back, and let me show you how it's done." Eye-Gore stuck his arms out in front of him and walked forward slowly, dragging his feet zombie-style. "Muuust eeeeat braaaaiin!" he moaned.

"Wow!" a fat man at the front of the crowd cried, turning on his video camera. "This stuff is great!"

"Okay, show's over," Eye-Gore said, dropping his arms. "These people wear plaid shorts and sandals with black socks," the zombie whispered to Bonehead. "No wonder they aren't worried I'll eat their brains—they don't have any!"

Horror stared at the crowd from the bathroom window. "They aren't leaving," he said to Willy, who was dozing peacefully on his knee. Horror was surrounded by all his swamp friends. The featherless birds were perched on his shoulders, and Coco was curled inside her bottle, tucked neatly away on the top shelf of the medicine cabinet. "What if they come inside?" Horror cried. "What if they want to use the bathroom? Some of you could get flushed away!"

But just then, a cheery tune floated up to the window.

How can I resist you,
When you smell so nice?
You may be kind of crusty,
But you're also filled with spice.
Oh! Pepperoni pizza! Pepperoni pizza!
I just want to gobble you up!

It was Frankie who was singing. He had returned from the water park an hour before, after finding out that he was too tall to go on the water slides. He also hadn't had a swimsuit with him.

When Frankie had seen the crowd outside

the Manor, he had grabbed his guitar and gone out to entertain them. After all, Frankie was a singer. In fact, he had a successful career as a recording artist. . . . He was known as Mister-E-Us. He'd had two top-ten hits, and he was very big in Japan, even though no one there had ever seen Mister-E-Us's face. Or maybe he was big *because* no one had ever seen his face.

Just as Frankie started to launch into the song's chorus, There was a loud shout of *"Aiiieee!"* and the professor, who had managed to climb up the gate, jumped onto Frankie's head.

Hey, Professor! Do you want an autograph?

No autographs!

That didn't hurt Frankie in the slightest. In fact, it was the professor who felt a little woozy, after bouncing off Frankie's head and landing on the ground.

"Are you okay?" Frankie asked. He helped the professor up.

"Don't be an idiot!" the professor said. "Do not zing for zeez people! Zey haven't given you any money for conzert tickets!"

"But I like to sing," Frankie protested.

The professor sighed. "Frankie," he said patiently. "Ve don't vant anyone to know vhat Mister-E-Us looks like, remember?"

"Why not?" Frankie asked.

Professor Von Skalpel didn't want to tell Frankie that it was because he was ugly, so he came up with a little white lie. "Because it is a secret. You are like . . . uh . . . like Batman."

"Oh," Frankie said, his eyes growing wide.

"Batman." He nodded, and hurried into the house.

"Boo!" The crowd jeered from the other side of the fence.

"Bring back the guy with the guitar!" shouted one woman.

"Yeah!" agreed her husband. "We want the guitar guy. We're bored."

"Now, everyvone just please calm down," Professor Von Skalpel said.

"Hey, that guy climbed over the fence!" shouted a man with a mustache. "He didn't even wait his turn."

There were more boos, and then a thin old woman launched her Whirl lollipop at the professor. He ducked, but not in time—the lollipop hit him square in the side of the head. Suddenly, everyone in the crowd started throwing things at the professor. Before he

knew it, the Manor lawn was covered with Whirl pens, stationery, cups, earmuffs, pairs of underpants, beach balls, plastic toys, and lollipops.

"Let's throw more stuff!" some guy shouted, and soon the crowd was launching handfuls of pink gravel through the iron bars.

The professor, Bonehead, and Eye-Gore ran into the Manor. But Kneecap spotted something in the pink gravel that had been tossed into the yard. It was a slightly different shade of pink, and she recognized it right away.

"My ribbon!" Kneecap shouted. But she didn't have time to reach for it, because just then, her mother dived behind her, scooped her up, and carried her into the house.

The crowd had started to claw at the gate. "We want mon-sters! We want mon-sters!" the people shouted. They pressed up to the gate—and it looked as though it would break at any minute!

Suddenly there was a loud roar, and everyone stopped shouting. What was that horrible noise?

Everyone turned, and when they saw what was behind them, they couldn't believe their eyes. It was huge. It was horrible. It . . .

CHAPTER NINE
The Thing That They Saw

. . . . **W**as the Bulldosaur. And D. K. Pitt was at the controls.

"Out of the way!" he shouted, like a maniac. "Out of the way!"

The crowd parted, and the Bulldosaur drove up to the Manor gate. A little man in a green suit trotted behind the Bulldosaur. He was carrying something that looked like a remote-control device.

Beatrice ran out of the Manor, followed by

Count Snobula and Steve. Beatrice was holding a piece of paper as though it were a shield. "You're on private property!" she screamed. "Get out of here, or I'll call the police!"

"You are being very rude," the count said.

"Get out of here, losers!" Steve added. He was grouchy because he wanted to get back to the video game he'd been playing.

The owner of GPC pulled the Bulldosaur's brake and climbed down. "Beatrice Monster?" he asked, ignoring Count Snobula and Steve.

"It's Mon *Staire*," Beatrice said.

"Whatever," Pitt said. "I knew your mother. Before she died, Sally sold me all of the land around the Manor."

"So I hear," Beatrice said. "But that doesn't make any difference. You may have bought all of the land around the Manor, but you didn't buy the land beneath it, or the house itself. I have the deed right here," she added, holding out her paperwork.

Pitt's smile didn't falter. "The house, yes . . . well . . ." He cleared his throat. "I've had some testing done, and it seems that there are two hundred and sixty-three highly toxic, illegal chemicals that have shown up on this land. I'd like you to meet Mr. Meddle, from the Transylvaniaville Department of Environmental Protection."

"Your property is a health and environment

hazard," Mr. Meddle said to Beatrice. "So I've given Mr. Pitt approval to go ahead with his project."

Beatrice scowled at the little man. "What does this mean?"

Pitt smiled a smile that sent a shiver down Beatrice's spine. "It means that I can demolish your Manor and build you a nice, new house. Don't worry, you'll be able to live in the new place, and it won't cost you a cent. Of course, you will have to put up with thousands of tourists stomping through. . . ."

"You're bluffing," Beatrice said to Pitt.

Mr. Meddle held up his machine. It was letting out several high-pitched chirps.

"What is that?" Beatrice asked.

"It's SNOT—the Scientific Notifier Of Toxicity. And SNOT never lies," Mr. Meddle said. "This place is so toxic, I can't believe we are still alive! This is unheard of!"

"Or un-dead," Steve whispered.

"Mr. Pitt, demolish this building at once!" Mr. Meddle commanded.

The owner of GPC turned to climb back into the Bulldosaur.

"Vait!" someone shouted.

Professor Von Skalpel shot out of the Manor, followed by Horror, who was holding a rather large box.

"Vait! Pitt is the polluter!" the professor shouted as he ran up to Mr. Meddle. "You're making a huge mistake!"

Mr. Meddle stared as the jellylike swamp creature set down a crate of mutant beasts.

"Ribbit," said Willy the toad.

"Have you ever seen animals like zis before, Mr. Meddle?" the professor demanded.

"Er—no," Mr. Meddle said. Then, under his

breath, he added, "Thank goodness."

"Of course not," Professor Von Skalpel went on. "Because zey only live in zee schvamp behind the Manor. Or, rather, zee schvamp that *used* to be behind the Manor—before Mr. Pitt ruined it vith his Bulldosaur!"

Willy blinked three of his eyes at Mr. Meddle.

Mr. Meddle gulped. "Are you saying that these creatures are . . . endangered?"

"Exactly," the professor said.

"Don't listen to him!" Pitt shouted. "He's

crazy! He's the one who polluted the swamp in the first place, with all of the waste from his illegal experiments."

Professor Von Skalpel ignored Pitt, and simply pulled a blue plastic Whirl toy from his pocket. "Mr. Meddle, vould you mind schcanning zis viz your machine?"

Mr. Meddle dangled SNOT over the plastic dolphin. SNOT started beeping like crazy. Smoke poured from the machine.

"What is that?" Mr. Meddle demanded, staring at the blue plastic. "It's the most toxic thing in the universe!"

"Zis," the professor said, glaring at Mr. Pitt, "is a toy sold at Vhirl Vorld. It's made of the same schtuff that everything at the park is made from. I just analyzed it in my lab. That's how Mr. Pitt 'fixes' his pollution problem—he just uses the Bulldosaur to turn toxic vaste

into plastic—and pink gravel!"

Mr. Meddle glared at Pitt. "This changes everything, Pitt," he said. "You won't be demolishing anything. And I'm going to get an order of protection for these endangered creatures!" he added, pointing to Horror's crateful of swamp beasties. As if to back up his statement, Mr. Meddle's machine started to make several high-pitched beeps.

Pitt started to laugh.

"You may think the beeping is funny," Mr. Meddle said, holding out his machine, "but it's SNOT. And when this thing goes off, it means that you blew it, Booger."

CHAPTER TEN
Bye-Bye, Whirl World

"You can't stop me!" Pitt shouted.

"Oh, yes, we can," Beatrice said, taking a step forward.

Pitt pulled out a stun gun.

"Then, again," Beatrice said, backing up, "maybe we can't."

"Destroy the monsters!" the crowd shouted. They had been watching the whole thing, and they thought this was just part of the show. Half of the tourists had out their video cameras and were taping away.

Beatrice, the professor, Horror, Count Snobula, and Steve stood there, frozen in fear. The other monsters watched from the Manor windows.

"Do something," Fibula said to Wolf Man Stu. "You're so fast that you could grab the stun gun out of Mr. Pitt's hand before he knew what was happening!"

"Sure," Stu said with a shrug. "But I'd rather watch the show."

All of the monsters clustered close around the window to see what would happen—all of them, that is, except for Frankie, who had mysteriously disappeared. . . .

Pitt turned to climb back into his Bulldosaur. But Horror couldn't let him go—not without a fight. Horror took a wet, splattery step forward.

He had a scowl on his face as he stared at Pitt.

"Hold it right there, Lumpy!" Pitt shouted, turning the gun on Horror. "Or I'll make mud pies out of you!"

But Horror kept on walking toward Pitt. He concentrated on keeping the scowl on his face.

"I'm warning you!" Pitt shouted. "I'll shoot!"

Horror took another step toward Pitt.

Pitt's finger trembled on the trigger, but with one quick motion Horror reached out and grabbed his weapon.

The crowd burst into applause.

"Way to go, Monster!"

"The blob is brave!"

"Oh, no! My video camera is running out of power!"

Disarmed, Pitt ran toward the Bulldosaur.

"Stop him, Horror!" Von Skalpel shouted. "He is getting avay!"

"Slime him!" Beatrice said. (She could be a little harsh, sometimes.)

But Horror didn't do either of those things. He knew something that the others didn't—he knew that what he held in his hand wasn't a weapon. It was just an old musical lighter from his box of treasures. He'd recognized it right away.

Horror ran for the Bulldosaur, but Pitt reached it first. He shifted the levers, and tried to bring the snapping jaws down on Horror's head, but the swamp monster was too quick for him. He leaped into for the driver's seat, shoving Pitt aside.

The crowd cheered again, even though they couldn't exactly see what was happening. The Bulldosaur windows were completely covered

You'll never catch me, barf bag!

in a thick, gross, green goo.

Horror shoved at one of the levers with his foot, and the Bulldosaur zipped toward the lake. The crowd quickly divided, jumping and diving out of the way.

"Not the lake!" Mr. Meddle shouted, but it was too late. The Bulldosaur had already tipped forward into the clear liquid.

Glub, glub, glub, went the machine as it sank beneath the lake. An odor much like a month-old tuna-fish sandwich smothered in crusty sweat sock filled the air as the toxic waste from the Bulldosaur's tank seeped into the clear water. . . . turning it back into a sickly, glowing green.

The Bulldosaur had drowned.

"Help!" came a cry from the toxic swamp. Pitt, his dark glasses askew, was paddling for shore.

"Where is Horror?" Bonehead asked.

"I really hope he wasn't trapped in the Bulldosaur," Steve said.

The monsters were silent, scanning the surface of the water for their friend.

"There he is!" Kneecap shouted suddenly.

Horror surfaced a few yards from the Manor, and spouted a stream of toxic water.

Willy and the other swamp beasts knocked over their crate and wriggled, flopped, and crawled toward the water. Coco turned her bottle over and rolled in.

"Ick! Phew!" the crowd cried as the smell from the swamp reached them. They high-tailed it away in all directions.

Horror grinned as he watched them go.

"Wait! Don't leave!" Pitt shouted. "The dolphin show starts again in twenty minutes!"

"There won't be any dolphin show," Mr. Meddle announced. "I'm taking Whirl with me. No wonder he seemed sick—you've been keeping him in a tank full of toxic toys! It's a miracle that he managed to pilot that helicopter at all!"

Just then, a police car pulled up. Tibia Femur had called 911 from the Manor. The policemen escorted Pitt into the backseat and drove off with their sirens wailing.

Horror leaned back·in his comfy swamp, happy to be surrounded by his little friends. He had never really realized how much that toxic water meant to him until it all nearly disappeared. Best of all, he had found his box of treasures—it hadn't been destroyed after all. It had been slightly crushed by the

Bulldosaur's gears, but the treasures inside were still all right. Horror smiled. Now he knew that everything was going to be okay.

"Velcome home, Horror," the professor said.

Horror grinned at him. "It's good to be here."

The rest of the monsters came pouring out of the Manor to congratulate Horror.

"It's good to see this slime again," Eye-Gore said.

"It does give the place a certain ambience," Count Snobula agreed.

"And smell that swamp air," Beatrice put in. "I could stay out here all evening."

All of the monsters agreed that that was a good idea.

"I found my pink ribbon!" Kneecap cried happily as she came running over to the group. "It was buried in all the gravel."

"That's wonderful!" Horror cried, giving her a big grin.

Just then, Frankie stuck his head out of the window. "Hey!" he shouted. "I finished cleaning the bathroom!"

The monsters stared at one another for a moment, and then they grinned and raced off for a much-needed shower.

Hey, there's only so much slime a monster can take.